21st Century Junior Library

PERSISTING WHEN THINGS ARE DIFFICULT

Building My Social-Emotional Toolbox

Emily Rose

Published in the United States of America by:

CHERRY LAKE PRESS
2395 South Huron Parkway, Suite 200, Ann Arbor, Michigan 48104
www.cherrylakepress.com

Reading Adviser: Beth Walker Gambro, MS, Ed., Reading Consultant, Yorkville, IL

Photo Credits: © Rawpixel.com/Shutterstock.com, cover, 1; © Lopolo/Shutterstock.com, 5; © Mariia Korneeva/Shutterstock.com, 6; © New Africa/Shutterstock.com, 7; © Milan Ilic Photographer/Shutterstock.com, 8; © Dragon Images/Shutterstock.com, 9; © Naypong Studio/Shutterstock.com, 10, 11; © MNStudio/Shutterstock.com, 12; © wavebreakmedia/Shutterstock.com, 13; © Juana Nunez/Shutterstock.com, 14; © AboutLife/Shutterstock.com, 17; © Pressmaster/Shutterstock.com, 18; © Efetova Anna/Shutterstock.com, 20; © Mix Tape/Shutterstock.com, 21 [top]; © Leonid studio/Shutterstock.com, 21 [bottom]

Cherry Lake Press is an imprint of Cherry Lake Publishing Group.

Library of Congress Cataloging-in-Publication Data

Names: Rose, Emily (School psychologist), author.
Title: Persisting when things are difficult / by Emily Rose.
Description: Ann Arbor, Michigan : Cherry Lake Publishing, [2022] | Series: Building my social-emotional toolbox | Includes bibliographical references and index. | Audience: Grades 2-3
Identifiers: LCCN 2022005325 | ISBN 9781668909065 (hardcover) | ISBN 9781668910665 (paperback) | ISBN 9781668913840 (pdf) | ISBN 9781668912256 (ebook)
Subjects: LCSH: Determination (Personality trait) in children—Juvenile literature. | Determination (Personality trait)—Juvenile literature. | Persistence—Juvenile literature.
Classification: LCC BF698.35.D48 R67 2022 | DDC 155.4/19—dc23/eng/20220214
LC record available at https://lccn.loc.gov/2022005325

Cherry Lake Press would like to acknowledge the work of the Partnership for 21st Century Learning, a Network of Battelle for Kids. Please visit http://www.battelleforkids.org/networks/p21 for more information.

Printed in the United States of America
Corporate Graphics

CHERRY LAKE PRESS

CONTENTS

NO ONE IS GOOD AT EVERYTHING (IT'S TRUE!)

LeBron James is very good at basketball, but he might not be as good at ballet. We are all good at some things and not as good at other things. It can take time to learn what we are good at, or more importantly, what we even *like* doing!

What's something you are good at?

Brianna's aunt plays the flute in a local **orchestra**, and she is really talented. Brianna felt **inspired** by her aunt. She tried to teach herself to play the flute but realized she doesn't like playing the instrument. She just likes to listen to music.

Trying new things is how we learn what we like. Sometimes, we learn what we don't like in the process!

What new thing have you been wanting to try?

Brianna was disappointed in herself and asked her aunt for advice. Her aunt told her, "Brianna, it's okay if you thought you might like something, tried it, and decided that you didn't. It's okay to try things and not like them. Trying things is the only way to learn what you *do* enjoy. Go ahead, and keep trying things until you find what you like!"

Think!

Think of a time when you were learning something new. How did it feel? Did you want to give up at times? Are you glad you kept going? What do you think you could learn from that experience to help you in the future?

PERSISTING—ESPECIALLY WHEN IT COUNTS

When we are not so good at something, or find it to be really hard, we may feel frustrated and want to give up. No one has to be good at everything, but there are things that everyone should keep trying hard to learn. These are life skills we need, such as reading, counting money, and being kind to people.

Make a Guess!

What is one important thing that you think everyone should know how to do? What do you think would happen if everyone quit trying before they learned how to do it?

To keep trying when things are hard is called **persistence**, and it's a great thing to practice. If we quit trying to learn how to read or tie our shoes just because it's hard, then we'll never be able to read a great book or run without tripping over our shoelaces!

Nathaniel found math to be so difficult that he did

Create!

Make yourself a note or a sign with words of encouragement to look at when you are working on something hard.

everything he could to **avoid** learning it. When his friend Mary saw him drawing a picture instead of practicing his multiplication tables, she asked him, "Nathaniel, don't you want to learn how to multiply? It's hard, but learning to add wasn't easy at first, right?" Nathaniel thought about what Mary said and knew she was right. He opened up his math book and said to himself, "I can do this. I learned to add, so I can learn to multiply too."

Not everything will be easy at first. But persistence pays!

STRATEGIES TO HELP YOU PERSIST WHEN THINGS ARE HARD

When you do hard things, it's also okay to take breaks. In fact, it's recommended!

Jamal's dad is an **expert** golfer. He plays for fun and to **compete** with other golfers. Jamal wanted to learn the sport so he could one day play golf with his dad. He asked for golf lessons for his birthday but had no idea it would be so hard. Each lesson is different and hard in many ways.

Sometimes, Jamal learned about the rules of the sport. Other times, he practiced how to hold and swing the golf club.

Jamal started to feel **discouraged** that he would never be as good as his dad. He talked to his dad, who told him something important. "Son, I've been playing golf for 14 years now. When I first started,

Look!

Look around to find examples of people trying really hard to learn something new. Maybe a friend in class is working hard on an art project or a baseball teammate is practicing his swing. Noticing the hard work it takes to learn something new can make you realize that learning new things is not easy for most people.

Who motivates you to keep going?

I felt frustrated all the time. Sometimes, I even felt like I would *never* learn how to play. You know what I did? I practiced one thing at a time, took a lot of breaks along the way, and reminded myself that learning takes time."

Taking a break is one great idea that can help you keep going when things are hard. Another thing to try is finding a buddy to **motivate** you to keep going or to ask for help. Reaching a goal is always easier when we have someone by our side!

Where do you find inspiration?

You can also look for inspiration to spark some positive feelings about pushing through difficult things. If you are trying to run a mile, you might research stories about people who run marathons and their tips for getting started. Finally, you can name your feelings and make time to sit with them. It might sound silly, but simply saying, "I feel frustrated" or "this is hard" and taking time to process how you feel can help you **acknowledge** and work through your feelings.

Ask Questions!

The next time you are working through something that feels really hard, like a long book report or learning to play an instrument, ask yourself, "How do I feel right now?" If you feel a negative emotion, like frustration or anger, you can choose one of the skills we talked about, like taking a break. If you feel a positive emotion, like feeling proud of yourself, take a minute to celebrate your hard work!

EXTEND YOUR LEARNING

Real-life challenge! Think of something that you are working on that feels very difficult. Maybe you are trying to get to the next level in a video game or learn a new language or long division. Make a list of some strategies to help you keep going! They could be strategies from this book or ones you think of on your own. Once you're done with your list, show it to a friend or adult and ask if they have other ideas that might help. Then add those to your list. Now you've got some great ideas to help you persist!

GOAL

GLOSSARY

acknowledge **(ik-NAH-lij)** to recognize or admit to be true

avoid **(uh-VOYD)** to steer clear of or not participate in

compete **(kuhm-PEET)** to participate in a contest or game

discouraged **(dih-SKUHR-ijd)** felt a lack of confidence

encouragement **(en-KUHR-ij-muhnt)** providing inspiration or confidence

expert **(EK-spuhrt)** someone with a special skill or knowledge in an area

inspired **(in-SPY-uhrd)** felt encouraged to do something

motivate **(MOH-tuh-vayt)** to encourage to do something

orchestra **(OHR-kuh-struh)** a group of people who play musical instruments together

persistence **(puhr-SIH-stuhns)** to keep doing something in spite of difficulties

FIND OUT MORE

Books

Murphy, Frank. *Stand Up for Responsibility.* Ann Arbor, MI: Cherry Lake Publishing, 2020.

Rose, Emily. *Recognizing and Managing Stress.* Ann Arbor, MI: Cherry Lake Publishing, 2022.

Rose, Emily. *Setting and Achieving Positive Goals.* Ann Arbor, MI: Cherry Lake Publishing, 2022.

Websites

YouTube—Habits of Mind: Persistence
https://www.youtube.com/watch?v=mAkwmomM62s
Watch this clip about persistence.

YouTube—Perseverance for Students
https://www.youtube.com/watch?v=IOaFwwLyTRo
Watch this video to see an example of perseverance and trying something new.

INDEX

ABOUT THE AUTHOR

Emily Rose is a school psychologist, yoga teacher, and writer for her mental wellness blog, MissMagnoliaSays.com. She enjoys helping kids and adults understand and manage their emotions and live beautiful lives. Emily lives in Dearborn, Michigan.